The 7th Night of July

Illustrated by Ke Ming and Huang Peizhong

English adaptation by Paula Franklin

Silver Burdett Company
Morristown, N.J. and Agincourt, Ontario

Once upon a time, many stars lived along the
Milky Way. They were ruled by the Lord, who
always watched gently over them.

A star named Vega lived on the eastern side of the Milky Way. She was a weaver-princess, who wove beautiful fabrics from morning till night. The click-click of her loom could be heard all day long.

Altair was a star who lived on the western side of the Milky Way. He was a farmer-prince, who tilled his fields from morning till night. He took good care of his ox, who pulled his plow.

On the eastern side of the
Milky Way, Vega did nothing
but weave. On the western
side, Altair did nothing but till
the fields with his ox.

8

The fabrics Vega wove were more gorgeous than clouds in the evening glow. And the rice Altair grew sparkled more than silver.

9

One day the Lord seated Vega on a cloud and carried her to the other side of the Milky Way. "Look at the star seated on a flower and playing the flute."

Vega saw Altair for the first time. He shone more brightly than the sun, yet he was gentler than the moon.

The Lord moved Vega to the western side of the Milky Way and married her to Altair.

Vega and Altair were very happy. She saw nothing
but him, and he heard nothing but her voice.

From morning till night the blissful couple
looked at each other and smiled. Sometimes Vega
danced while Altair played his lute.

Vega and Altair were so happy that they forgot
all about the ox and the loom. Altair's ox grew
thin and weak, and weeds overran the rice fields.
Vega's loom gathered dust, and mice skittered
about the weaving room.

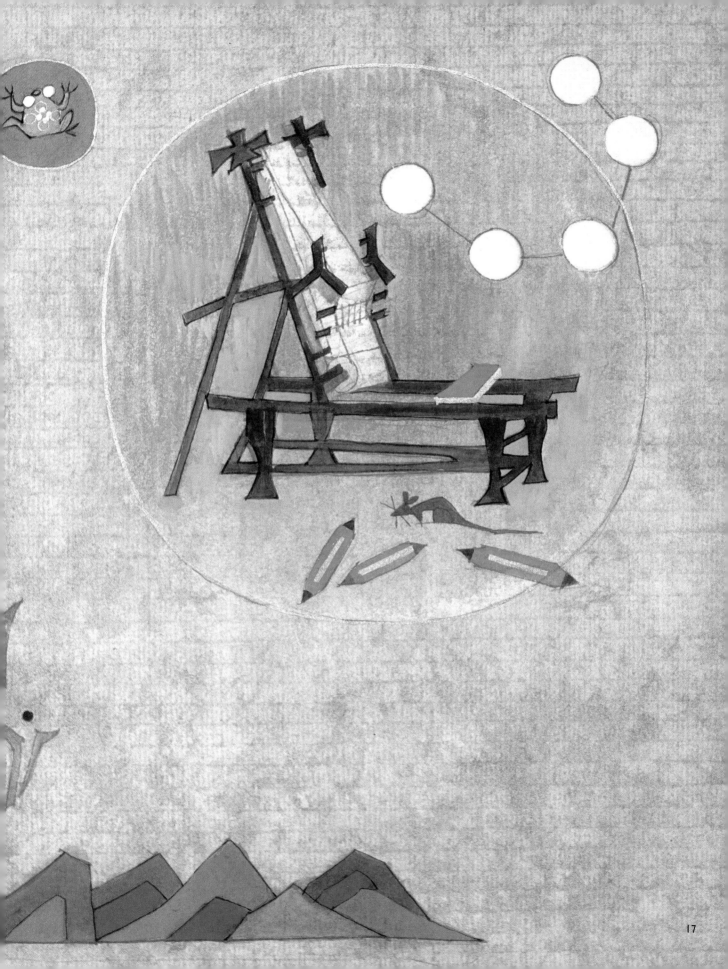

The Lord chided them several times. "Vega, weave your cloth. Altair, look after your ox and your fields."

"Yes, yes, we'll go to work tomorrow," the two would reply. But tomorrow would come and go without any work done. In this way ten days passed. A month went by. The ox grew weaker, the loom dustier.

Now the Lord's anger boiled over. He separated the two stars, taking Vega back to the eastern side of the Milky Way. "From now on," he said sternly, "you must live apart. But if you work as hard as you used to, I will let you meet once a year."

Since then, the two stars have obeyed the Lord, and they meet once every year—on the seventh night of July. On that night, thousands of magpies gather at the Milky Way. They form a bridge that Vega crosses to meet Altair.

"Altair, Altair, I'll soon be there," cries Vega as she crosses the bridge. Altair waits on the western side, his heart beating wildly, as his sweetheart approaches.

The two hold hands and look into each other's eyes until daybreak. Vega sees nothing but her beloved. Altair hears nothing but the voice of his sweetheart.

On the next seventh of July, try to find a grape arbor. If you stand under it, you will hear the happy laughter of Vega and Altair.

STORIES FROM · · AROUND THE WORLD ·

The 7th Night of July ©1983 Gakken Co., Ltd., Tokyo
Adapted and published in the United States by
Silver Burdett Company, Morristown, N.J.
1985 printing
ISBN 0-382-09047-0
Library of Congress Catalog Card Number 84-40798
Depósito legal: M. 8504-1985
Edime, S. A. - Móstoles (Madrid)
Printed in Spain

About the Artists

Huang Peizhong is a Designer for the Nantong
Institute of Arts and Crafts in Jiangsu Province,
China.

Ke Ming is an art editor for the Jiangsu People's
Publishing House, in Nanjing, China.